W9-AVM-279

MAGIC CASTLE READERS®

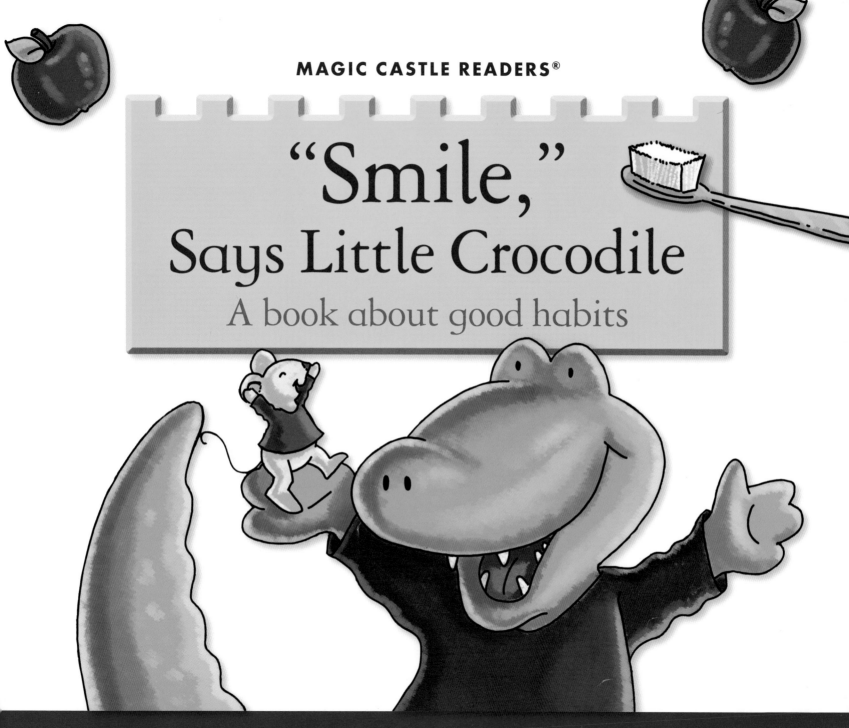

"Smile,"
Says Little Crocodile

A book about good habits

BY JANE BELK MONCURE • ILLUSTRATED BY SUSAN DeSANTIS

The Child's World

Published by The Child's World®
1980 Lookout Drive • Mankato, MN 56003-1705
800-599-READ • www.childsworld.com

Acknowledgments
The Child's World®: Mary Berendes, Publishing Director
The Design Lab: Design
Jody Jensen Shaffer: Editing
Derrick Chow: Color

ISBN 9781623235703
LCCN 2013931411

Printed in the United States of America
Mankato, MN
July 2013
PA02177

Did you know...

A library is a magic castle with many Word Windows in it?

What is a Word Window?

If you said, "A book," you're right!

A book is a Word Window because the words and pictures let you look and see many things. Books are your windows to the wide, wide world around you.

The Library
Is a Magic Castle

Come to the Magic Castle
When you are growing tall.
Rows and rows of Word Windows
Line every single wall.
They reach up high,
As high as the sky,
And you'll want to open them all.
For every time you open one,
A new adventure has begun.

Tess opened a Word Window.
Here is what she read:

"I like to smile," says Crocodile.

"When I smile, guess what I see.
A smile comes smiling back at me."

"The doctor helps me keep my smile,"
says the little crocodile.

"She keeps me well from head to toe.
My smile gets bigger as I grow."

"Good food helps me keep my smile,"
says the little crocodile.

"I eat apples and celery for snacks and treats instead of too many gooey sweets."

"Exercise helps me keep my smile,"
says the little crocodile.

"I jog. I climb. I jump rope, too."

"I like to hike and ride my bike.
Exercise keeps me smiling all day through."

"Another way I keep a smile is by dressing
for the weather," says Crocodile.

"I wear boots and a snowsuit in the snow,
so I stay warm from head to toe."

"Sniffles and sneezes take smiles away,
so I try to stay dry on a rainy day."

"Another way I keep my smile is by visiting the dentist," says Crocodile.

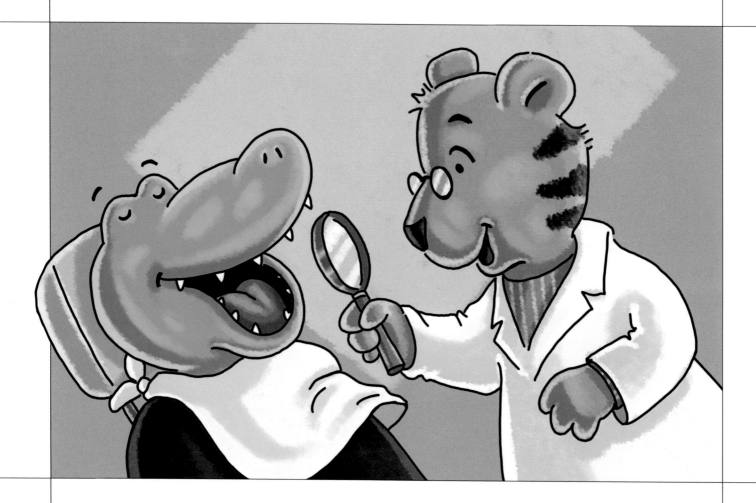

"I open my mouth very wide
to let the dentist peek inside."

"He cleans my teeth so they look new.
And my crocodile smile comes shining through."

"A toothbrush is a smile's good friend.
I brush my teeth from end to end."

"I brush my teeth row-by-row,
just the way they grow."

"I brush up from the bottom and down from the top. Then around in circles before I stop."

"I take care of my health the whole year through."

"That is why my crocodile smile
is the happiest, snappiest smile of all."

"Here is how you can have a happy, snappy
crocodile smile:

Visit the dentist.

Brush and floss your teeth.

Visit the doctor.

Eat healthy food for snacks.

Dress for the weather.

Exercise every day. All these things will help you
stay well and be happy inside!"

Questions and Activities

1. In one sentence, tell what this book is about.
   Name three ways the author tells the book's main idea.

2. Describe the little crocodile. Write two things about the crocodile.

3. Who is telling the story?
   How does the little crocodile feel about smiling?

4. Did this story have any words you don't know?
   How can you find out what they mean?

5. Name two things you learned about having a happy smile.
   What else would you like to know about?